Tractor Day

Candice F. Ransom

Illustrations **by** **Laura J. Bryant**

Walker & Company
New York

Text copyright © 2007 by Candice F. Ransom
Illustrations copyright © 2007 by Laura J. Bryant

First published in the United States of America in 2007 by
Walker Publishing Company, Inc.
Distributed to the trade by Holtzbrinck Publishers

For information about permission to reproduce selections from
this book, write to Permissions, Walker & Company,
104 Fifth Avenue, New York, New York 10011

Library of Congress Cataloging-in-Publication Data
Ransom, Candice F.
Tractor day / Candice F. Ransom ; illustrations by Laura J. Bryant.
p. cm.
Summary: Simple rhyming text describes a child's day spent riding on the tractor with
Daddy at their small farm.
ISBN-10: 0-8027-8090-3 • ISBN-13: 978-0-8027-8090-4 (hardcover)
ISBN-10: 0-8027-8091-1 • ISBN-13: 978-0-8027-8091-1 (reinforced)
[1. Tractors—Fiction. 2. Farm life—Fiction. 3. Father and child—Fiction. 4. Stories in
rhyme.] I. Bryant, Laura J., ill. II. Title.
PZ8.3.R1467Tr 2007   [E]—dc22   2006013642

Book design by Nicole Gastonguay

Visit Walker & Company's Web site at www.walkeryoungreaders.com

Printed in China

2 4 6 8 10 9 7 5 3 1

All papers used by Walker & Company are natural, recyclable products
made from wood grown in well-managed forests. The manufacturing processes
conform to the environmental regulations of the country of origin.

For Howard and his famous Ford
tractor —C. F. R.

To Ruel, Ernie, Freel, Elwood,
and Hoy —L. J. B.

Black birds perch,
dance on gate.
Hello, crows.
Don't be late!

Tractor naps.
Time to plow.
Cover off.
Wake up now!

Leather seat.
Noisy gears.
Up we go!
Daddy steers.

Motor coughs.
Sprockets whir.
Tractor starts.
Rrrr! Rrrr!

Lower hitch.
Hear it grind.
Tractor drags
plow behind.

Chomping tires.
Brown mud churns.
Round and round
tractor turns.

Big wheels roll.
Blade makes rows.
Overhead,
watching crows.

**Plow bites deep,
digs up things.
Broken cups,
rusty springs.**

Tractor rests.
Leafy shade.
Waiting crows,
unafraid.

Tractor stirs.
Vroom! Clatter!
Unhitch plow.
Crows scatter!

Hook up disk.
Lever down.
Metal plates
chew up ground.

Sun is hot.
Take off shirt.
Harrow's teeth
rake the dirt.

Tractor stops.
Time to plant.
Packets, seeds.
Look out, ant!

Black birds swoop.
Beady eye.
Strut and peck.
Off they fly!

Corner tight.
Tractor stalls.
Try again.
Plot too small.

**Marigolds,
zizzing bee,
little patch
just for me.**

Tractor chugs
back to shed.
Good night, crows.
Time for bed.